For Peter and Jemma—*A. B.*
For my niece Tung Hei (Winter Morning Sun)—*M. S.*

First United States edition 1995
Text copyright © 1995 by Antonia Barber
Illustrations copyright © 1995 by Meilo So

All rights reserved including the right of reproduction in whole or in part in any form.

Macmillan Books for Young Readers
An imprint of Simon & Schuster Children's Publishing Division
Simon & Schuster Macmillan
1230 Avenue of the Americas
New York, New York 10020

Copyright © 1995 by Frances Lincoln Limited

First Published in Great Britain by
Frances Lincoln Limited, 4 Torriano Mews
Torriano Avenue, London NW5 2RZ

Printed and bound in Italy

10 9 8 7 6 5 4 3 2 1

Library of Congress Cataloging-in-Publication Data
Barber, Antonia.
     The monkey and the panda /Antonia Barber ; illustrated by Meilo So. —
1st U.S. ed.
         p.   cm.
     Summary: Differences triumph and the imagination is celebrated in
this fable about a monkey jealous of a panda beloved by all the children.
     ISBN 0-02-708382-9
     [1. Fables.   2. Monkeys—Fiction.   3. Pandas—Fiction.] I. So,
Meilo, ill.   II. Title.
PZ8.2.B194Mo 1995
[E]—dc20   94-33001

THE MONKEY AND THE PANDA

ANTONIA BARBER

Illustrated by MEILO SO

Macmillan Books for Young Readers • New York

Long, long ago, to the east of the sunrise, there once lived a Monkey and a Panda. Monkey was lean and lithe and lively. Panda was fat and furry and friendly.

The children of the village loved them both. When they played, they loved Monkey, who was noisy and naughty and made them laugh. When they grew tired, they went seeking Panda, who was quiet and comfortable and soft to sleep upon.

But Monkey grew jealous of Panda, for he thought the children loved her more.

Each day his tricks grew wilder as he tried to keep the children laughing. His antics caused havoc in the village, until the villagers longed to be rid of him. But they were gentle people and did not wish to harm him.

Close by the village lay a ruined temple. The monks had
gone away into a far land, all but one wise old man who
was too frail to cross the high mountains. The people of the
village brought him food and cared for his needs,
and in return he gave them his wisdom.

When they told him of Monkey's terrible tricks,
the old man smiled.

"Master," they said, "it is no laughing matter!"

"No, indeed!" said the old man, straightening his face.
"I see that you have a real problem. Bring Monkey to me
and I will talk to him."

The people came, bringing Monkey, who was cross and sulking.

"Set him down," said the old man gently, "and leave us alone together." Then he asked Monkey why he had grown so troublesome.

"It is all Panda's fault," said Monkey.

"How can that be?" asked the old man. "For Panda eats and sleeps in the bamboo grove and harms no one."

"What you say is true," said Monkey, "and yet the children love her. However hard I try to make them laugh, sooner or later they go to her. Yet judge between us, Master, if I am not better in every way!"

The old man thought a while. Then he said:

"Is it a judgment you seek? Would you have one better and the other worse? If so, we must see what Panda has to say for herself."

He lifted Monkey onto his shoulder and set off to the bamboo grove where Panda lived. And the children, who were hiding among the ruins, stole after them.

They found Panda sitting in the middle of the grove, eating bamboo shoots.

The old man greeted her and she nodded in return. But she did not speak, for she had good manners and her mouth was full.

"You see," said Monkey, "she has nothing to say for herself."

"Panda, my friend," said the old man, "I have come to judge between you and Monkey, who is worthier."

Panda went on chewing peacefully, and if she was surprised by their mission, she did not show it.

"Each shall speak in turn," said the old man, settling himself on the ground. And the children hid among the tall stems of the bamboo grove to see what would happen.

The Monkey could not wait to begin.

"I am better than Panda," he boasted, "because there is nowhere that is not mine. From the tallest treetop to the forest floor, all is my kingdom. I can climb, I can swing, I can leap, I can fly—well, almost. But as for Panda, she just sits in the bamboo grove all day long and never goes anywhere."

Panda said nothing. She listened to the rustle of the leaves
all about her. She watched the pale sunlight as it broke through
the mist. It seemed to her that the bamboo grove was the loveliest
place in all the world.

"I am more cunning than Panda," Monkey went on.
"I find fruit in the treetops, take eggs from the birds' nests,
smell honey in the hollow tree. I am even smarter than
the villagers, for I trick them out of their food."

Panda said nothing, for her mouth was full of young green leaves. They were fresh and crisp and sweet on her tongue. It seemed to her that the bamboo shoots had the most delicious taste in all the world.

"You must admit that I am more fun than Panda," said Monkey. "My tricks make the children laugh, my daring makes them gasp. I am bolder and braver and a great deal livelier. Compared to me, Panda is boring."

Still Panda said nothing—for she had fallen asleep. She
dreamed of the sunlight and the green leaves quivering
in the wind and the taste of the bamboo shoots on her
tongue. And it seemed to her that her dream was the
best dream in all the world.

Now Monkey grew desperate and his boasting grew ever more fantastic.

"I can ride on the clouds," he cried. "I can speed with the wind. I can travel over the mountains to the world's end. Why, I have fought with dragons and rescued princesses!"

When they heard this, the children stole out of the bamboo
grove and gathered silently around him.

Then Monkey told them a long tale of magic and
monsters, of his brave deeds and bold rescues. As he talked
he held the children enthralled and watched their dark eyes
grow wide with wonder.

But if you ask me, Was it all true? I can only tell you that these things had happened in Monkey's dreams, and so, in his dreams, they *were* true.

As the children listened they remembered their own dreams, which they had forgotten upon waking; Monkey gave their dreams back to them.

When Monkey's story ended, the children clamored for more.

But the old man hushed them, and turning to Panda said, "Panda, you too must speak, if I am to judge between you and Monkey."

Then Panda woke with her dream still about her, and out of her love for the bamboo grove, which was her home and her life, she spoke at last. Her voice was as soft as the wind stirring the leaves, and she said:

"Whisper in the wind, shelter in the storm,
catching the sun's gleam in the mist of dawn.
Crisp in my mouth, sweet on my tongue,
you become me, we become one."

And the children, who had played all their lives in the
bamboo grove and had never really noticed it, looked up
at the moving leaves outlined against the sunlight and
saw them truly for the first time.

The old man watched and smiled, and he said, "How rich our lives have become! Monkey has taken us to the ends of the world and Panda has shown us into the heart of it. Who am I to judge between them?

Cherish Monkey, my children, for he is a very great storyteller, and honor Panda, for she is a poet."